Tracy and the Heroes in Blue

Written by
Janet Dobson

Illustrated by
Jon Stuart

Illustrations by Jon Stuart

Photograph of Janet Dobson by Jonae Steinman

Published by Miriam Laundry Publishing Company
miriamlaundry.com

PB ISBN 978-1-990107-55-9
e-Book ISBN 978-1-990107-56-6

FIRST EDITION

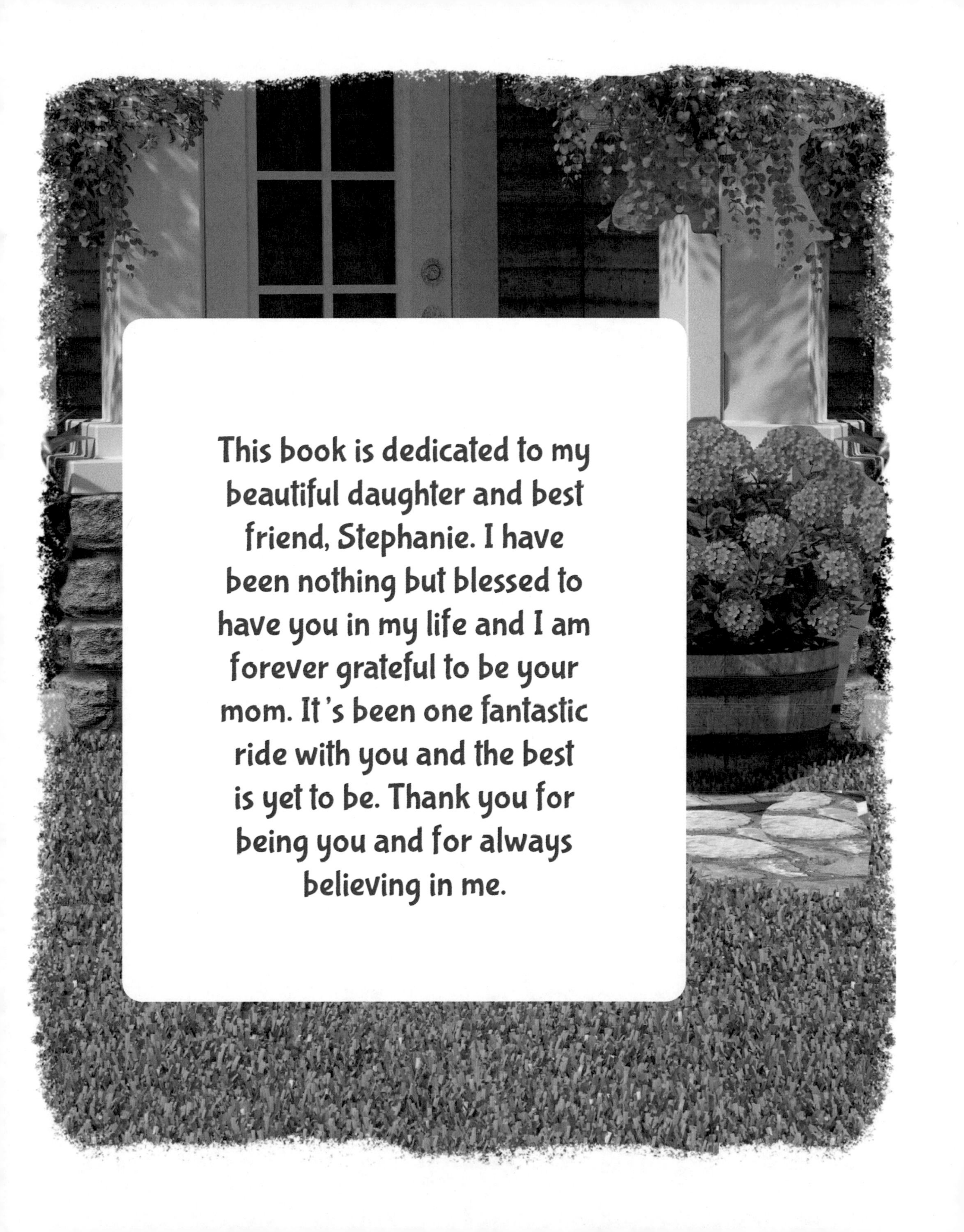

This book is dedicated to my beautiful daughter and best friend, Stephanie. I have been nothing but blessed to have you in my life and I am forever grateful to be your mom. It's been one fantastic ride with you and the best is yet to be. Thank you for being you and for always believing in me.

Tracy and her mom pulled into the driveway. It had been six weeks since Tracy left home for the hospital. As soon as Tracy opened the car door, her friend Marie ran outside to greet her.

"Tracy, Tracy!" exclaimed Marie. "I missed you so much!" Marie stared at her friend in confusion. "What happened to your hair?"

Tracy, who had been smiling, put a hand to her head. Her shoulder length strawberry blonde curls were no longer a part of her. "Chemo made my hair fall out," Tracy explained sadly.

"Chemo?" Marie questioned.

"Chemotherapy or chemo for short. But my hair will grow back."

Marie still looked confused.

"I have leukemia," Tracy said. "It's a form of cancer. That's why I was so tired before. So I had to stay in the hospital for treatment," she groaned. "It wasn't fun."

"I'm glad you're back." Marie gave her friend a huge hug.

The girls smiled at each other as Tracy's mom came back outside.

"Tracy, are you tired?" her mom asked with concern. "Maybe you should lie down and rest before dinner."

"After all the sleeping I did in the hospital? I'm not tired at all!" Tracy told her mother. "Can Marie come in and play on my new tablet with me?" She pulled a brand new tablet out of her bag.

"Wow!" exclaimed Marie. "How did you get that?"

"The Roc Solid Foundation® gave it to me," Tracy said.

Her mom added, "When we got to the hospital, we didn't have everything we needed. We didn't know we'd be there for a whole six weeks."

"So these really nice people gave me a Ready Bag with all kinds of neat things in it," Tracy said. "And this tablet was like my best friend."

"Hey!" Marie pretended to pout.

"My best friend when you weren 't there," Tracy laughed. She turned to her mom. "So can Marie and I play?"

Her mom thought for a minute and then hesitantly replied, "Okay, but only for a little while, and after you both wash your hands. We have to be extra careful now about germs."

The girls rushed to wash their hands and then Marie asked, "Tracy, did it hurt when they gave you chemo?"

"Not too much." Tracy pointed to a small scar on her chest. "They attached this thing called a port and gave me chemo through it. That meant I didn 't have to get stuck with needles."

"Were you scared?"

Tracy frowned. "It was scary at first and sometimes I was sick to my stomach. But the doctors and nurses were really nice and took good care of me. And after my immune system got stronger they even let me play in the playroom with the other kids."

"So now you 're all better?" Marie asked hopefully.

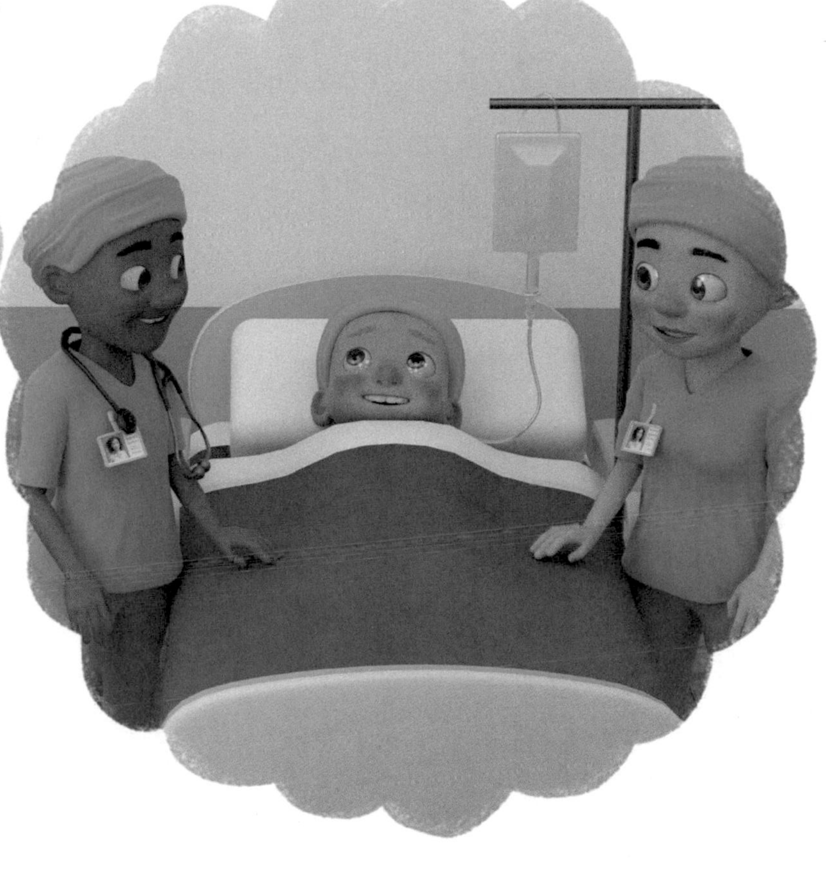

"Not yet, but the doctors say I will be. I still have to take medicine and have lots of tests done."

Just then Tracy's mom poked her head into the room. "Marie, your mom wants you home for dinner."

Marie jumped up. "I'm glad you're back, Tracy. Everyone at school misses you."

"The doctors said I can go back to school." Tracy grinned. "I can't wait to see all my friends!"

Tracy's mom frowned. "Now sweetie, you know I said we'd have to discuss you going back to school. Your health is still fragile."

Tracy sighed. As she walked her friend to the door, she glanced over at the shelf displaying her mom's collection of porcelain dolls. She wasn't allowed to play with them. They were 'for show only,' her mom always said.

"You know what?" Tracy whispered to Marie. "My mom is treating me like one of those dolls. Like I'm breakable!"

The next morning the sun shone brightly through Tracy's window. For a moment she thought she was still in the hospital. But when she remembered, she quickly bounded out of bed.

After breakfast she saw Marie riding her bike. "Mom, I 'm going out to bike with Marie!"

"Not so fast sweetie. I think you should take it easy today and ..."

"Mom, I don 't want to take it easy! I want to play! You 're treating me like one of your dolls!" Tracy exclaimed with anger.

Then she saw tears in her mother's eyes. "Mom, I know you're worried about me but I'm not made of porcelain. And you know the doctors told me I could play like I used to."

"You're right sweetie," her mom whispered softly. "But I still worry about my baby girl."

"I know, Mom," Tracy said with a smile, giving her mom a big hug.

"I've got an idea!" her mom exclaimed.
"Why don't I take you and Marie to a movie?"

Tracy agreed and ran to tell her friend.

"Let's go right now," her mom insisted.
"We can catch the early movie."

"But..." Tracy began.

"No buts. Let's go!" Tracy's mom hurried the two girls into the car just as a big truck was pulling up in front of the house.

"Are they coming here?" Tracy asked.

Her mom shook her head. "Must be for the neighbors," she answered.

They all enjoyed the movie. It was wonderful to sit in a theater again and eat a big bag of popcorn. But it wasn 't quite as wonderful as the surprise Tracy got when she arrived home.

Tracy could hardly believe her eyes! In her backyard was a beautiful play set and lots of people wearing blue shirts. She recognized some of them and remembered the big truck and suddenly figured it out.

"Roc Solid!" she exclaimed. "You built this for me?"

"They sure did sweetie," declared her mom, choking back tears.

"Wow! I love it!" Tracy screamed with excitement.

"Some days you won 't be well enough to play at the park with the other kids," her mom explained. "This will give you a safe place to have all the fun you want."

"Thank you everybody!" Tracy told all her friends from the Roc Solid Foundation®. She and Marie ran for the swings. "Thank you for letting me play."

Tracy would still need more treatments and doctor visits. But for that moment, outside and playing with her friend, no one was thinking about cancer.

About Roc Solid Foundation®

Roc Solid Foundation® is a nonprofit that builds hope for families fighting pediatric cancer. Founded by pediatric cancer survivor Eric Newman, the organization is best known for surprising kids fighting cancer with backyard playsets and providing Roc Solid Ready Bags to families when they first hear the news of their child's diagnosis. More than 16,000 kids are diagnosed with cancer in the US each year, and Roc Solid's vision is to one day build hope for every single one.

The author would like to thank Roc Solid for their support of her in the making of this book.

For more information, visit www.rocsolidfoundation.org

About the Author

Janet Dobson is a mother, entrepreneur, real estate investor and devoted volunteer for the Roc Solid Foundation® (RSF). As a cancer survivor herself, Janet understands the importance of organizations such as the RSF. She has seen firsthand how the RSF is making life-changing impacts on families fighting pediatric cancer. Janet wrote *Tracy and the Heroes in Blue* as a part of her mission to show these families what hope looks like and that they are not alone on their journey. This is her first published book. She happily resides in Virginia Beach, Virginia when she is not adventuring around the world with her daughter Steph. You can come along with Janet on her adventures by visiting her website janetdobson.net and following her on Facebook and Instagram.

@ janetsdobson

Made in the USA
Middletown, DE
18 May 2022